This book belongs

_____

Copyright © 2017, 2021
By Ariane O'Pry Trammell
All rights reserved

First edition, 2017
First Pelican edition, 2021

The word "Pelican" and the depiction of a pelican are trademarks of Arcadia Publishing Company Inc. and are registered in the U.S. Patent and Trademark Office.

ISBN: 978-1-4556-2610-6

Printed in Korea
Published by Pelican Publishing
New Orleans, LA
www.pelicanpub.com

DEDICATION

This book is dedicated to

The Trammell Family.

Push-polin' t'ru the bayou in dat ole pirogue
was Boudin, T-Boy, and dat gator, Fais-Do.

Dey drop in the swamp all dem crawfish trap.
Dey catch 'em all up and dey put 'em in a sack.

"Aye! Aye! Ayyye!" T-Boy yell,
almost comin', out the boat,
When a wily lil' crawfish done snap his big toe!

Boudin laughed, "Couillon! Das a crazy one d'er!"
as he done plop back in the water
flippin' roun' his derrière.

"Dey sure don't wanna mess wit' me!
Dey'll get a big surprise!"
said Couillon, dat lil' crawfish wit' the crazy in his eyes.

Life as a tasty mudbug...
It can get a little rough.
I gotta be a fast one,
and I sure gotta be tough!

A big ole bird might come along and try to snatch me up!

A large mout' bass could swim on by and eat me wit' one gulp!

Dem crafty river otter would find me a scrumptious treat,

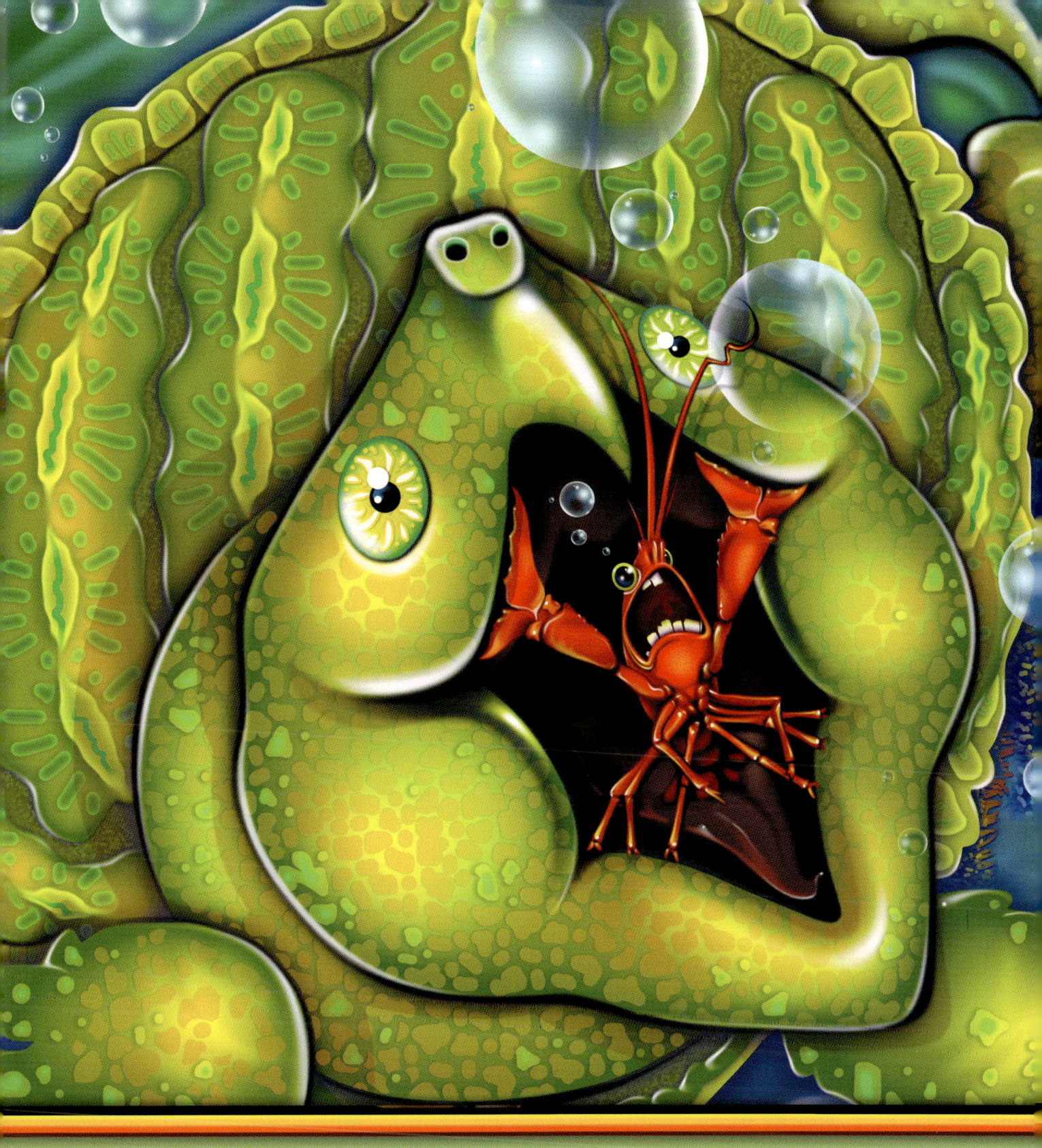

And dat alligator snapper sho' enough would chomp on me!

But, boy, I gotta tell ya,
the most fearsome beast of all...

Is dem hungry, happy Cajuns
when dey have dem crawfish boil!

D'er we'll be, jus' scootin' along
and mindin' our own bidness,

Den stop to have a little snack,
and das jus' when dey get us!

Sack us up and take us home
and put us in a boilin' pot,

Wit' garlic, potato, corn, and all dem other lil' fixin's dat dey got.

As if dat ain't been bad enough,
dey pinch our lil' tail,

Suck our heads, eat us up,
and give a crazy Cajun yell!

"Ahhh-eeeeeh! Dem crawfish sho' taste good!"
as dey have a belly full of 'em
at a festive family fais do-do,
and everybody's comin'.

Ya Paran, ya Nanan, ya Pop-Pop,
and Mamou . . .
Dat lil' ole lady up da road,
and ya Mama-n-'em comin' too!

A lucky few of us will manage to escape,

And others might become a pet, if only for a day.

Now, I'm a little spicy!
I'll put up a good fight!
I'm Couillon, dat little crawfish
wit' the crazy in my eyes.

Go have ya'self some gumbo,
jambalaya, or fricassee.
Make up some étouffée,
but no one's eatin' me!"

About the Author/Illustrator

Ariane O'Pry Trammell is an artist and children's book author/illustrator from the small town of Ponchatoula, Louisiana. Having illustrated numerous publications for other authors, whom she guided through the process of self-publishing, she was encouraged to write a children's book of her own. Her first book, *Where the Grass Is Always Greener*, was released in 2013.

As the mother of two young sons, Kellan and Gavin, Ariane is constantly inspired to create. Often featured in her illustrations, her children are even depicted as the characters Boudin and T-Boy in her very successful Cajun series. She launched the first book of that series, "*Run! Boudin, Run!*", in 2016. *Cicada's Song* soon followed in 2017. *Couillon, the Crawfish* made its debut in 2018.

Ariane finds herself immensely blessed to have a career that is both her passion and a God-given gift. She is a member of the historic French Market in New Orleans, where she regularly sells her books, and she often visits schools and libraries to share her stories. She hopes to inspire, encourage, and instill a love of reading and art in every child.

Find the author online:
www.ArianesArt.com

Facebook.com/ArianeTrammellBooks

To schedule an event with Ariane, contact her directly:
artbyariane@hotmail.com